THE DEAD OF THE

The

Murray Bar

Case

By

Julie Burns Sweeney

Copyright: 2017

Published by: Lulu.com

ISBN: 978-0-244-91165-2

CHAPTER ONE

Murray studied Leah Trueman carefully. She looked older than her twenty-seven years, a couple of grey hairs already appearing within her auburn fringe and the first sign of crow's feet at the sides of her brown eyes. The telling signs of worry? How was he going to tell her that there wasn't a great deal he could do for her? Ali and Rita had made it clear in the past that suicides couldn't be contacted after death and they should know about these things, being on that side of life themselves. Sometimes he believed that not having the 'gift' of hearing the dead would make life so much easier. Still, here he was sat in Leah's kitchen, listening to

3

her heart-felt plea that she must know why her sister had ended her life.

"I'm not sure how I can help you Miss Trueman. I understand that this must have been extremely upsetting but..."

"Mr Barber please. There's more to this than what you first see. I believe this started six years ago when Lauren and six of her friends camped on the beach for the night, except they didn't end up staying on the beach. Something terrible happened and Lauren, and the other's, were never the same again."

"Oh?" Murray sat forward, leaning his forearms on the edge of the table. "Why don't you start from back then, then, and tell me the whole story?"

"They were all about sixteen, seventeen. There was

Lauren, Clare Alexander, Hannah Clark, Jasmine Wills, Chantelle Stevens, Abigail Pengellis and Nicole Sampson. They were typical teenagers and to be honest, Mum thought it would be all girls and boys together that night. She interrogated Lauren no end before she went but she insisted there would only be the seven of them, NO boys! I drove down to the front at about ten-thirty that evening just to check and believe it or not, there weren't any boys! Generally speaking, Lauren was a very honest girl."

"So what happened?" Leah had stood up and poured out two coffees on the worktop behind her. She then sat back down at the table with Murray while continuing.

"I don't really know. Lauren wouldn't talk about it. None of them would say. She came bursting back in the door at about midnight, white as a sheet. She went straight up to bed and just wouldn't say anything. We thought they'd probably started telling ghost stories and freaked out! Thing is, she's never been the same since. She always looked haunted and nervy. And she'd never tell us what happened. The other girls were pretty much the same, except for one, Nicole. We never saw her again, apparently, she ended up in hospital that night and the next thing, her parent's moved away. She had cut her wrist open. She bled to death... Dead. I don't know what they were doing that night but it was a dangerous game."

  "And you think that has haunted your sister all these years and now she's finally given in and killed herself? That would mean she was guilty of something surely?"

"Maybe? I just want to know what happened that night."

"Can't you just ask the other girls?"

"I'm not sure where they are now, and I'm not sure they would talk to me anyhow? That's why I thought of a private investigator. I can see on your face you think I'm on a foolish mission. I know what I find out will probably hurt but at least I'll know. I need to understand whether it was guilt or part of a suicide pact that the girls all agreed to?"

"Excuse me, I don't want to sound offensive, but doesn't that sound a little far-fetched?"

"On its own yes, I expect it does. But you see, last year Chantelle killed herself and before that, Hannah did too...."

Murray sat back in his car outside Leah's townhouse, it was a new car, an Astra. After his crash up on the moor two months previously, his Mondeo had been a write-off. The courtesy car they had provided he hadn't used. How could he follow someone without looking conspicuous in a lime green logo-covered Golf? He'd woken up in hospital, well, he'd drifted in and out of consciousness for a couple of days and then regained his faculties. One of his first thoughts had been whether or not he had lost his 'gift'? But he was sure, pretty sure, he had heard the sound of a flute playing while he had drifted in and out of sleep. And once he had been left alone during the night, Ali and Rita had spoken up and asked him

8

how he was. 'Glad to still be alive' had been his reply. One fractured rib, which was still very tender, and a lot of bruising had been a lucky escape. The whole experience had also prevented him from making a massive mistake. He hadn't made that phone call to Michelle. He still hadn't spoken to her two months later. Hopefully she would have assumed that he had changed his mind, like she had said herself, if he wasn't comfortable with cheating on Jenny....

So now life was getting back to normal, the jobs were trickling in, at least this one now sounded a little more intriguing than the usual 'follow my unfaithful spouse'. He started his engine and turned over in his mind what Leah Trueman had just told him about her sister, Lauren's, death. She was only twenty-two but had spent the last six years becoming more and more withdrawn and 'tortured', Leah's word, until finally she had seemed mentally ill and overdosed on sleeping tablets and paracetamol. It sounded very tragic. It also sounded somewhat worrying considering two of the other girls had also committed suicide in the last eighteen months. Was it just a coincidence? Or was it linked to six years ago and a possible pact between the girls which would mean there were more deaths to come? The first thing he needed to do was track down the whereabouts of the surviving girls and then ask Ali and Rita to see if they could track down any of the dead girls?

So once home, with coffee at his side, the laptop was turned on and the searches began. The girls were only in their early twenties and so hopefully not married yet. He first tried Jasmine Wills whom he found straight away living just across the river. He noted down her address and telephone number before trying Clare Alexander. As he waited for a result his phone rang, it was his mother.

"Hi Mum, how are you?"

"Nothing wrong with me dear, just checking up on you. How are the aches and pains?"

"I'm fine Mum. I've been good for a couple of weeks now, so stop worrying!"

"I can't, I'm your mother! But I'm glad to hear it anyway. Look, I was thinking, why don't the two of you come down for Sunday lunch? Jenny won't be working Sunday will she and I know you can shift your hours around when you want to?"

"Erm.. I'll have to run it past Jen first but I'm sure she'll say yes. What time do you want us?"

"I'll dish up at one so whenever you like."

"Ok, we'll see you then, bye Mum."

Back on his screen, an address and telephone number had come up for Clare, she only lived five minutes away. He glanced at the clock in the corner of his screen, it was five forty-five. Perhaps time for a takeaway and then he'd try Clare first as she was nearer. He'd better not leave it too late however, they were both still young enough to be out on the razzle on a Friday night.

As he strolled around the corner to the Chinese, Jenny text a message to his mobile. She had been there everyday since his accident, either in person or on the phone. From the moment her flight had managed to land from Tokyo in all that bad weather until today, she had been worse than his mother worrying about him. Being honest with himself, Murray knew it only made him feel worse for misbehaving behind her back but he promised himself that she would never find out and so never be hurt by his actions, she deserved better than that. She told him to get a duck in plum sauce and a side of rice and she'd join him back at his flat. It brought a smile to his face and besides, she might just be able to help him with this 'girl-pact' case....

CHAPTER TWO

Jenny sat back and ran her fingers through her hair, it was blonde again now with a few light-brown low-lights running through the length of it, and then reached for her glass of Merlot.

"It sounds so sad that these girls are killing themselves, you just can't imagine what could have happened that night to make them want to do this to themselves?"

"No." Murray shook his head. "I'm about to try and call two of the surviving girls, it'll be interesting to hear what they have to say... assuming that they'll talk to me that is." He picked up his glass and turned to Jenny. "Do you believe this 'no boy' stuff about that night? Surely girls of that age would have invited boys?"

"Well, you would have thought so wouldn't you? I hope this doesn't turn out to be one of those times when things got out of hand, if you know what I mean?"

"Uh, yeah. Hadn't thought of that. Mind you, there were seven of them, surely it would have taken quite a few boys to turn that situation nasty? And..." he waved a finger as he put his glass back down onto the coffee table. "... the time frame only allows about an hour. Half-ten this Leah says she drove down to the beach and her sister was home around midnight."

"True, it doesn't sound long but how long do these things take? And something, whatever it was, did happen. Do you know exactly what happened to that girl that died?"

"Er.. Nicole? No, not really. Just that she cut her wrist and died and then her parents moved away."

"Did she cut it on the beach or when she got home? Did she get home even?"

"Don't know? Leah wasn't all that clear. I suppose they didn't find out about her straight away? Hopefully one or other of these three that are left will be willing to tell us? Suppose I better try phoning, pass me my notebook..." Jenny handed him over the small, scruffy notepad and Murray dialled the first number.

"Hello, can I speak to Clare Alexander please?" he asked.

"Oh yes, speaking."

"Hello Clare, my name's Murray Barber, you won't

16

know me I'm a private investigator and I've been hired by a lady called Leah Trueman to look into the death of her sister..."

"Her sister? Lauren? Is she dead?"

"I'm sorry. You didn't know?"

"No, no I didn't." The voice at the end of the line sounded shocked and quite upset.

"I'm sorry I've had to break it to you like this. It was a few weeks ago now. You did know her then?"

"I knew her yes. Lauren. We were at school together, but I haven't seen her in ages, years. How did she die?"

"I'm afraid she killed herself." The line was silent. Murray couldn't hear any sobbing and the phone hadn't been hung up. He waited a moment for Clare to take in what he had just said before continuing.

"Erm... I'm very sorry. I was hoping you could tell me a bit more about Lauren. You say you haven't seen her in years?"

"No. No, I haven't. Not since.... " Again there was silence.

"Not since when?" Murray was hoping that Clare herself might just bring up the beach camp.

"Can't really remember."

"Would it have been a certain beach party? About six years ago?" If she didn't want to co-operate Murray would just have to encourage her.

"Oh, that's a long time ago. I... I don't really remember. Is there anything else you wanted to ask?"

"Well, it was mainly about that night on the beach. Do you think I could leave you my number and if you do happen to recall anything, perhaps you could give me a ring?"

"Oh... ok then." She sounded a little relieved. Murray gave her his number, although he wasn't completely convinced she wrote it down, he could only hope she might just change her mind. Either way, he didn't want to alienate her during their first conversation.

Jenny raised her eyebrows.

"The conspiracy continues to evolve! I take it she didn't want to talk about it?"

"Not really." Murray shook his head. "Well, we'll just have to hope we can catch her in a better mood tomorrow. I'm not giving up that easily! Now let's try the other one.. what's her number?" Murray took another mouthful of wine and then dialled

Jasmine's number as Jenny read it out to him.

"Hello, could I speak to Jasmine Wills please?"

"Hang on. Jazz!" The male voice shouted out. "She's just coming."

"Hello?" She finally asked after Murray had heard her reprimand the male voice for not finding out who it was.

"Hello. My name's Murray Barber, I'm a private investigator. You won't know me, I've been hired by Leah Trueman. I'd like to ask you some questions if I may about her sister, Lauren?"

"Lauren?" Jasmine sounded surprised. "Yeah, I remember her! Haven't seen her in ages though."

"No, she seems to have lost touch with her old school friends. I take it you haven't heard what happened to her?"

"No?"

"I'm sorry to have to be the one to tell you, but I'm afraid she died..."

"Damn! How come? She's only my age."

"Well, her sister says she hasn't been the same since you all went on a camp night at the beach, some six years ago? And lately she'd become very depressed and finally took her own life."

"Damn! Yeah I remember that night. It was a long time ago now mind? Surely she had got over it?"

"It would seem not. Is there any chance I could ask you about that night?" This sounded more hopeful.

"Erm... well, does it have to be now? It's just I'm getting ready to go out?"

"No. No it can wait. Are you free at all tomorrow?" There was a pause before she answered.

"OK. Can we make it about three? I'm out for lunch first."

"Sure that would be great. Shall I come to yours?" Murray put a 'thumbs up' at Jenny.

"Do you have my address?"

"Yes, I have it here."

"Ok, see you tomorrow then. Bye Mr Barber."

"Success!" beamed Jenny.

"Well I wouldn't say that, not yet, but at least it's a step forward." Murray topped up the glasses and sat back. "Don't have much to go on do we?"

"You've got to start somewhere. Tomorrow will hopefully fill in more of the picture. You've got one more to trace haven't you? And what about the others? You know, the ones that have died? You say they were suicides as well? What about speaking to their families?"

"Good point. Yep, I'll have to look them up tomorrow, but not now, now I'm starting to get drunk....."

CHAPTER THREE

Murray woke up with a slight hang over on Saturday morning, something he never used to suffer so easily before the crash. Still, the aroma of bacon coming from the kitchen roused him from the bed and he headed into the bathroom for a quick shower. He was hoping Ali and Rita would show up sooner rather than later. He wanted to ask them to go in search of the three dead girls, whether they were suicides or not. It was a pity he didn't have a direct line to the 'other side'.

Freshly showered, he strolled into the kitchen and gave Jenny a gentle kiss on the nape of her neck.

"Mmm, that smells good."

"It's only bacon, eggs and mushrooms. Couldn't find any tomatoes. Look, I've got some notes and stuff to sort out before Monday, if I get on with that this afternoon, is that ok? We can enjoy your Mum's dinner tomorrow then without having to rush back?"

"Yeah, ok. I think I can handle this Jasmine on my own." He was teasing. So, after breakfast, Jenny headed off home to her house-share and Murray decided to give his old mate, Jeff from C.I.D., a call.

"Alright Jeff? How's Kate doing?" Kate, Jeff's wife was expecting their first child.

"She's fine, tired a lot of the time but at least we seem to have missed out on all this morning sickness lark they go on about!"

"Well give her my love. I've called to ask a favour."

"Oh? What is it this time?" Jeff, as usual, was in a good mood.

"I've just started this case involving a group of girls that went on a beach camp night about six years ago..."

"Sounds exciting!"

"Huh! Now they're committing suicide one by one. You couldn't run a couple of checks for me could you?"

"How many girls are we talking about? I can't say I

know anything about any such case?"

"There were seven girls. One died around the original night, six years ago, and since then three more have committed suicide. I've been hired by the latest victim's sister to find out what happened that night."

"It's starting to sound a bit gruesome. How old are these girls?"

"They were sixteen or seventeen. Early twenties now. Can you just check and see if there was any sort of an investigation six years ago? The girl's name was Nicole Sampson."

"Yeah, got that. I'll see what if anything it chucks back out at me. You ok are you?"

"Yeah. Everyone keeps asking! I'll be out visiting one of the surviving girls this afternoon and then I'll be at my Mum's tomorrow, so there's no panic.

Thanks again." He hung up and then jumped.

"Murray my man! You doing ok?"

"Not you as well Ali! I'm fine! All better thank you very much! Glad you've turned up, is Rita with you?" Murray glanced around his empty lounge.

"As always Murray babe. You in need of our services by any chance?" Rita's voice was young and light.

"If you've got nothing else on?"

"As if man! We just heard your conversation with Jeff, doesn't sound a very nice business." Ali was glancing at Murray across the top of his small round glasses, his hands shoved firmly down into his jeans pockets.

"No, I don't think it is." Murray stared towards the

kitchen door where Ali's voice was coming from. "I know you're gonna say you can't get in touch with suicides, but can you see if you can find anything out? Something strange is going on."

"Sure Murray, we can ask. But why are they just starting to kill themselves now? Six years later?" Murray stared at the armchair where, unseen by him, Rita sat twiddling with her long red ponytails.

"I hadn't thought about that Rita. It is a bit odd, isn't it?"

By the time Murray picked up his keys and headed out of the front door in the direction of Jasmine Wills he had managed to track down the last of the surviving girls, Abigail Pengellis, but she hadn't answered her phone so he planned to try again later. He'd also tracked the death certificates of Chantelle Stevens and Hannah Clark which had given him their last addresses and parent's details. He still had to trace back six years to look for Nicole's details, but that could wait till he returned from Jasmine's.

It was raining but only lightly as Murray drove west over the bridge across the river. Jasmine's house was easy enough to find although it turned out that she in fact, rented the top floor flat within a large terraced house.

Jasmine was a thin and pretty enough blonde, although wearing too much make-up for Murray's liking. Her straight hair hung almost down to her waist. She didn't seem at all upset by the death of her school friend, Lauren, as she slumped down on the window seat which gave onto a photographic worthy view of the busy river and bridges.

"Do you want a cup of tea Mr Barber?"

"That'd be nice if it's no trouble?" Murray took a seat on the settee and pulled out his trusty notebook. The flat was small, bathroom, bedroom and the kitchen/lounge area in which they sat. It wasn't particularly neat either.

"Excuse the mess, I've been doing some sorting out. I don't usually live in a pigsty." Murray smiled and hoped he hadn't shown a disapproving look upon his face, after all, he was hardly one to keep things tidy!

"Don't worry! You don't mind me asking about all this I hope?"

"No, not really." She handed him a mug and sat

back on the window seat. "I don't know exactly what you want from me though?"

"Can you tell me what happened on the beach that night?"

"Oh, back then?" She paused to sip her own drink and glance out of the window. "It was a bit of a laugh really. Or at least it was supposed to be! We arranged to have a sleep over down on the beach, it was going to be a warm night and there was enough of us not to panic the parents too much!"

"Who was there, do you remember?"

"Oh, me! Err... Abby, Hannah, Clare, Charlie, Lauren..."

"Charlie? Boys were there?"

"Oh no! Charlie's a girl! Chantelle. The boys were told to come back later. And Nicole was there of course."

"Hopefully we'll get to Nicole, but can you start at the beginning of the evening and tell me what happened?"

"I take it you heard what happened to Nicole then?" Jasmine was studying Murray's face closely.

"Not really, only that either that night or soon afterwards, she committed suicide?"

"Something like that. She didn't usually come out with us. To be honest, she was one of those girls that didn't fit in very well. She was going to be the butt of our joke, but it was only supposed to be a joke!" Again she paused and glanced out of her window. "We'd decided to get her to join us in a type of initiation game. No-one was supposed to get hurt. We were just going to have a bit of a laugh.

The lads turned up about half nine and we told them to clear off until later...."

"Which lads were these?" Murray was making notes.

"Tyler, Charlie's boyfriend, Mark, Abby's, and Ashley who was trying it on with Clare. Anyway, we had all cleared off before they came back, if they came back but I suspect they did. We hadn't planned on staying out all night anyhow, not really, maybe one or two in the morning and then head home."

"So what did this 'game' involve?"

"Looking back now, it was such a stupid idea." For the first time Murray saw a glimmer of regret in the girl's eyes. "We had this penknife, all we were going to do was make a small cut and perform a made-up 'blood pact'. It wasn't serious! A small cut across the wrist. Hannah went first, then Charlie, then Lauren, Clare, Abby, myself and then we handed the knife to Nicole."

"So it was an accident?" Murray had stopped writing and was staring at Jasmine questioningly.

"Stupid girl nearly sliced her hand off. We all freaked when the blood started gushing out. As far as I know everyone ran home, including Nicole. We wondered whether she had made it or not, then later when we heard she had died..."

"No-one took the poor girl home or called an ambulance or got any help...?"

"She was ok. She was on her feet, upset yes, but able to run like the rest of us. No-one wanted to get shouted at by her Dad, he was a great big bloke..."

"But you did see her head home?"

"Yes. We all felt bad, especially when we heard... you know? But it wasn't really our fault. We'd all managed to cut ourselves without doing any real harm. Personally I think she did it on purpose, for attention like, she was a bit of an oddball. Anyhow, I know I never saw her again and the rest of us tended to keep our distance from each other after that. It was a bit freaky and we just felt awkward around each other afterwards."

"And you didn't know about Lauren, or Hannah or Chantelle?"

"Hannah and Chantelle? Are they dead too? What all suicides?" Murray just nodded slowly but didn't say anything. "Damn! That is freaky! Weird? All because of Nicole? I don't think so, not because of that?"

"It's the only common factor at the moment but I've only just started looking into it."

"So who's hired you, Leah?"

"Yes. She just wanted to know what really happened that night so she could understand her sister. Apparently she was never the same again and started suffering from some form of mental health problem and finally overdosed a couple of weeks ago. I think Leah just wants some form of 'closure' as they say." With little more added to Murray's notebook, he left Jasmine to the rest of her day and headed back home, he still had some more research to do and a couple of phone calls to make.

CHAPTER FOUR

The rain came down as Murray returned home from Jasmine's flat. He managed to get himself soaked just running from his car in the resident's carpark to his front door. Once inside, he changed into his dressing gown and, noticing his answer phone flashing, checked his messages. There was just the one from Jeff.

"Sorry Murray, nothing on any Nicole Sampson. Nothing at all! Not six years ago or anytime since. Let us know if I can do anything else."

Not to give in so easily, Murray sat himself down and dialed Abigail's number, maybe she'd answer this time? It rang..... and rang. He hung up. Maybe she'd answer the next time? He took his notebook from his jacket pocket and flicked through until he found the numbers of Hannah and Chantelle's parent's. These weren't going to be the easiest of phone calls but he was determined to make contact with at least one more person. Hannah had died first, so he decided to start there and after explaining who he was and why he had called, Mrs Tina Clarke was very co-operative...

"... it was quite shocking how she changed. Initially, after the night at the beach, she was quiet but it didn't last. Then about two months before she died, she suddenly became... well, very paranoid. It really wasn't like her at all. At first we thought she was just stressed out, she had been working long hours and still going out lots but she stopped going out all of a sudden. To be honest, it all happened over such a short time. She became jumpy and she looked awful, really tired. I remember asking her if she was sleeping alright and she started rambling about seeing Nicky. I didn't realize who she was talking about at first but then, when she said about it again, she said Nicole. We said to her 'but she died didn't she?' but she just kept insisting she had seen her. She became quite obsessed about it. I dragged her along to the doc's in the end and he prescribed sleeping tablets. He said it sounded like sleep deprivation. The strange thing was, when they did the post-mortem, they found different sleeping drugs in her system along with a cocktail of other drugs, we never did find out where she got those from. Do you think there was something odd then Mr Barber? I mean, with all three of them dying, supposedly in exactly the same way?"

"I couldn't say for sure Mrs Clarke, but it does sound strange doesn't it? Considering they supposedly weren't in contact with each other. I think there's got to be a common denominator somewhere, I've just got to find it."

"If you do find out anything about Hannah's death, or any of the other's, could you please let us know? We still don't really understand what happened to our daughter."

"Of course Mrs Clarke. And if you think of anything else, please feel free to call me anytime, you can leave a message if need be."

Murray wasn't quite sure what to make of his

phone call with Hannah's mother. Why should the girl have changed so much so quickly? He wondered just what drugs she had been taking? And what was she on about 'seeing Nicole'? He felt he needed a chat with Ali and Rita. He was sincerely hoping this wasn't about to turn into another 'Keeley' type case where the dead wreak their revenge!

  Having paused to make himself a coffee, Murray once again made himself comfy, with pen and notepad handy and dialled Chantelle's parents.

  "...She was fine after that incident at the beach, she told me what happened and I did ground her for getting involved in something so stupid. Of course, once we heard the news that Nicole had died... can't remember who told us that? ... Never saw her again anyhow. Then I really laid it into her NEVER to do anything like that again, and she listened, I know she did. But then, well, I'd say it started a few months before her overdose, she changed. I thought she was taking something, you know? Drugs? Her personality changed. She was a nervous wreck, totally paranoid. Kept saying 'she's coming for me'. I tried asking who but all she would say was 'her, Nicole'. The girl had died like four years before, Mr Barber, Charlie was talking rubbish. She wouldn't go to the doctor. Wouldn't let anyone help her. I felt helpless. She just ranted about this Nicole and then... well, it was too late. She had traces of LSD and plenty of sleeping pills in her along with paracetamal. A deadly concoction Mr Barber."

   After the call ended Murray sat staring at his

notebook. It was almost an identical pattern. Two girls with two or so months of paranoia followed by overdose and death. And Nicole was responsible. But was she a vengeful spirit....

"Hello, Murray Barber, private investigator." His mobile had rang and he had automatically picked it up and answered with his usual message.

"Murray babe, it's me, Jenny."

"Oh hi hunny. Sorry, was trying to make the brain work! How are the notes coming along?"

"Erm... I'll get round to finishing them in a minute, look, I got thinking about this case of yours and I thought I'd look up the family of the girl that died on the beach that night... well not actually on the beach but you know what I mean. Nicole Sampson."

"Did you have any luck?"

"Well, I looked up the electoral role, you said they had moved away, and after a bit of searching and cross-referencing, guess what I found?"

"What? Although I think I might have an idea."

"She's not dead!"

Jenny had not only managed to track down the whereabouts of Mrs Sampson, Mr Sampson had left the family home, but had also found out that Nicole was not dead and had even managed to arrange a visit on Monday morning. So, Murray felt it was time for an 'update' call to Leah. If she had heard as much as she wanted, she may wish to pay him for what he had done and leave it at that. He certainly hoped she wouldn't, especially as he felt there was still a hint of danger for the remaining girls.

He dialed her contact number...

"Oh hi Mr Barber. Do you have some news for me?"

"Some yes. Your sister, along with the others had decided to play a bit of a stupid prank on that girl Nicole when they camped on the beach. They had a penknife, not sure who's it was, anyhow, they had this ham-brained idea of this blood-pact thing where they took turns in cutting their wrists and then supposedly joining blood. Something daft like that. That's when Nicole, who went last apparently, cut herself quite badly. Thing is, she didn't die..."

"She's not dead? But doesn't that mean when Lauren said she'd seen her...."

"Did Lauren see her aswell?"

"Yes, yes she said she did. I thought she was just

getting paranoid, you know, with the guilt. But if this girl isn't dead...maybe, well maybe she's responsible for the letters I've found..."

"What letters?" Murray picked up his pen and turned over a page in his notebook.

"I can give them to you if you like? They're not very nice. I've been going through some of Lauren's things and... well, there's no envelopes but there's about a dozen all spurting abuse about Lauren being evil and vile and stuff. She never said anything about them, I don't even know why she's kept them? You're welcome to have them if they're any help."

"You asked me to find out what happened that night on the beach, do you want me to continue?"

"Do you think there's more to this Mr Barber?"

"Well, the strange thing is, all three girls have died in almost identical circumstances. Have you had any results from a post-mortem yet?"

"Er, no. They did do one but I haven't asked anything about it, why?"

"It's just that both Hannah and Chantelle suffered from severe paranoia before they eventually over-dosed, but both were shown to have cocktails of drugs in their systems and both said they 'saw' Nicole. What did Lauren say about seeing her?"

There was a short pause before Leah answered.

"Mr Barber, please answer me honestly, do you think my sister was murdered?"

"Ah Leah, I can't say that. Not yet anyhow. If you want me to continue searching for evidence I will? We can then pass on anything we find to the police."

"Oh yes. Definitely. If there is a chance that either she was driven to this or actually murdered by someone, I want them punished. Lauren shouldn't have died just because of some stupid prank six years ago." Leah sounded almost angry. Sensing her emotion Murray thought better of telling her about the meeting on Monday arranged with Nicole's mother. He'd update her afterwards.

"Ok. I'll track down this Nicole and I'll also see if any of the surviving girls received any letters. I'll be in touch, ok?"

"Right Mr Barber. I'll scan these letters and e-mail them to you."

With Leah's phone call over, Murray sat back and tried to order his thoughts. What did he have so far? Seven girls on a camp night. One the butt of the 'joke'. It goes wrong and Nicole is badly hurt, but she doesn't die like the rest of them think. Four years or so later the girls start dying one by one having taken cocktails of drugs and supposedly been visited by the 'dead' girl. So what happened during those four or so years? What made Nicole decide to take revenge? And did she write the letters? Monday would be an interesting morning....

CHAPTER FIVE

Murray had picked Jenny up from her home and the two of them had driven down to the fishing town where his parents lived. The weather was being consistent, still drizzling and as they followed the coast road the sea mist hung in the damp air. They were met with the usual warm welcome and fussing. His parents had grown very fond of Jenny, Murray wondered whether they would have liked Michelle just as much, but it was only a glimmer of a thought that disappeared as quickly as it had formed.

With his Mother reassured, for the umpteenth time, that he had fully recovered from his crash, the conversation over dinner turned to the town gossip. There were all the usual flirtations and comings and goings of certain locals and the ups and downs of the local businesses. And then there was the funny business at the town museum.

"What's this then Mum?" Murray asked as he tucked into his Mother's 'local organic topside beef joint' and all its trimmings.

"I don't really want to bother you with it but well, Emma Walker, you know her don't you?"

"Always reminds me of an old-fashioned school headmistress!" Murray half laughed.

"Yes." His Mum frowned at Murray across the table and then continued. "Well, as I was saying, Emma came to me on Friday, caught me outside the post office, and asked about you..."

"About me?" Now it was Murray's turn to frown.

"Yes, she wanted to know if you were still working as a private investigator, they think they might be in need of your services."

"Really? She works at the museum?"

"Yes, she does a bit of everything there. Anyway, they think they've had an intruder..."

"Why don't they report it to the police?"

"They have but you see, nothing's been taken and it's not exactly Fort Knox! It's only local curiosities in there." She had turned to Jenny almost apologetically. "But someone's been disturbing things, sort of moving them about. She says, 'cos she knows absolutely everything in there, that when she opens up in the mornings, things just aren't quite in their right place. She says it's really a waste of the police's time but it's a bit unnerving."

"So nothing's been stolen, it's just someone sneaking in at night to have a bit of a snoop?"

"By all accounts dear, yes. Do you think you could help in any way? They are happy to pay." His Mum looked at him expectantly. Murray shrugged.

"Sure. I've got some surveillance stuff, cameras, I can set up in there for a couple of nights if they like. I'm not using them at the moment anyhow. I'll even do it for free, for the community!"

"Oh don't do that dear, they'll have you doing all sorts if you start offering your services for free! So I can give her your number then?"

"If you'd told me over the phone Mum, I'd have brought the equipment with me, I could've set it up this afternoon."

"Oh you are good." She picked up her empty plate and pecked him on the top of his head as she passed heading towards the kitchen.

They finished the dinner, which was appreciated by all, and retreated into the lounge where his Mum and Jenny sat watching the afternoon crime drama and his Dad, not wanting to head out in the rain to the pub, started to snooze in his armchair.

"Murray, can we have a word?" It was Rita's voice whispering behind Murray's armchair. Why she felt the need to whisper, he wasn't quite sure?

"This is a bit like 'busman's holiday'." He joked nodding at the tv. "I think I'll make that call to Emma, Mum. Have you got her number?"

"It's by the phone dear, in the hallway." Murray got up and headed out of the room and closed the door behind him. He picked up the phone and sat down on the stairs, but he didn't dial any number.

"Rita?" he whispered.

"Yes we're here Murray. We've been having some

fun trying to get hold of your girls."

"Don't tell me, you can't, they're suicides?"

"No man, well, yes and no. It's normally pretty black and white these things but sometimes it ain't, know what I mean?"

"No Ali, not a clue?"

"They were feeling suicidal but they didn't kill themselves." Rita tried to explain. "They were being manipulated. And there were lots of drugs being mixed into their foods which they didn't know about. Hallucinatory drugs. And then the final overdose."

"Who by?"

"Well, according to the girls, we've managed to reach a connection with Lauren and Chantelle, they both say it was Nicole who they saw in their houses."

"And we know you said she was dead Murray mate, but she's not on our side, she's still on yours."

"Ah yeah, I know. Jenny's tracked her down. She's taking me over to their house tomorrow."

"Oh good. Was that a waste of our efforts then?" Ali was laughing.

"No! No, not at all. It's always good to hear it from the horse's mouth as it were. It looks like we've got a dangerous young lady on our hands. Thanks you two."

"No worries man."

"You can meet us there tomorrow if you like, have a snoop around the house for us?"

"Where is it?"

"Not sure Rita. Better follow us in the morning."

"Ok. We'll leave you to your family get together!" Silence fell over the hallway, Ali and Rita having departed, so Murray dialed the number on the pad next to the phone cradle and got through to Emma Walker. She apologized incase she was wasting his time but he soon reassured her that it would be a simple job for him to install a couple of hidden cameras and if anyone did manage to get into the museum, well then they'd be caught on film and hopefully identifiable. She had sounded relieved and he arranged to come back the following afternoon, Monday after his morning visit to see Nicole, and set the equipment up. He then returned to the lounge for another hour or so telly watching and then headed home for a quiet night in with Jenny.

CHAPTER SIX

Jenny didn't have to go into work Monday
morning as both she and Gareth, her boss, were
taking the three twenty train to Edinburgh and they
weren't returning until Tuesday night. She had
stayed overnight at Murray's flat and now he woke
to the smell of bacon drifting into the bedroom
from the kitchen and the sound of Ali's flute playing
in the lounge. It was time he got up!

"You must get some shopping in. You've got no
eggs left or any fresh veg."

"Sorry." He smiled at her pathetically as she
handed him an unhealthy but delicious bacon

sandwich.

"So where does this Nicole live?" He asked as he carried his mug of coffee and plate into the lounge.

"Torquay. Do you want me to drive? I've got to be back in Exeter by two though."

"No, I'll drive and then I can drop you off on the way home..."

"You drive carefully!"

"Don't point your finger at me like that! It's not snowing! I'll be fine. What's the address?"

"Fleardon Road. Number twelve. It's near the seafront apparently."

"Oh right, should be easy enough to find then." His comment was aimed at all of those present. Ali's flute had stopped playing as the two of them had entered the room and now he answered Murray.

"Number twelve Fleardon Road. Righty-ho man!
Catch you there."

Murray was sure rush hour was supposed to end at

nine but even at ten the roads to Torquay were

heaving with traffic. It crossed his mind that maybe

there had been an accident somewhere causing a

detour and the traffic to merge but he didn't want to

switch on the local radio incase he was right. The

rain had stopped overnight but the roads were still

wet and the air was still damp, it was a pretty

miserable sort of day. Jenny was cheerful enough

though and threatened to buy Murray a kilt while

north of the border!

The Sampson house stood detached with large sea-

facing windows which could only afford those

inside a fantastic view. Murray parked up in front of the gate and with a 'well let's get this over with', the two of them approached the front door.

Mrs Sampson looked prematurely grey and held the two with a hard expression upon her face. This was followed by absolutely no sympathy at all for the three girls who had taken their own lives, or at least had officially done so. She was bitter about what had happened to her daughter and she evidently still held the other six girls responsible.

"Don't expect me to say 'oh dear what a shame'. If their guilt led them to harm themselves, well then that just serves them right. Nicole's life has been ruined since that night and our lives too." She hadn't offered them anything to drink and now sat on the edge of her armchair puffing away on a cigarette.

"We agree Mrs Sampson, those girls were totally out of order that night. From what we gather, they had decided to play out the scenario as a practical joke on Nicole." Jenny spoke in her most sympathetic tone, well trained from dealing with unhappy clients and bosses alike over the years she had spent as a PA. "Could Nicole give us her version of what happened that night? It's just that with the way these three have died, we want to make sure no-one else is at risk. How is Nicole? Has she recovered from the events or is she depressed or even paranoid?" Mrs Sampson didn't seem taken in by Jenny at first. She sat and studied Jenny through squinted eyes before letting out a loud sigh and stubbing out her cigarette in the ashtray.

"Look, my daughter doesn't even have a life. We took her to hospital that night and then, under advice from the docs, we took her for counseling. We honestly thought she'd been hiding something from us and tried to kill herself. We totally believed that and whatever she said at first we didn't listen to her. We even had her committed for a while to try and force her to open up. We did her more harm than good but we were only trying to help her.... it was them that started it. They made us believe there was a problem that wasn't really there. Not at first anyhow, even Nicole thought there was something wrong with her by the time we took her home. It got too much for Den, he took off on some job in Portugal. The only help we get from him now is money!"

"Is Nicole in, Mrs Sampson?" Jenny sat herself forward and Murray paused with his pen hovering above his notebook where he had been silently making notes.

"In? She's always in!" Mrs Sampson was mocking. "She never goes out. Agoraphobic. Hasn't been outside this house since we moved in. She doesn't want to talk to you though. She's hiding upstairs and that's where she'll stay till you've left. She doesn't like meeting strangers. Like I said, ruined her life. She may not have died that night but she's sure serving a life sentence. Been diagnosed with HIV as well now. She probably got that from that night too! Bloody girls, I could kill 'em! I don't care what you think of me, I'm glad they're suffering, I'm glad they're dead!"

"I'm, we're so sorry Mrs Sampson. And I'm sorry to have intruded into your privacy like this." Jenny glanced at Murray as Mrs Sampson lit another cigarette. He folded up his notepad and the two of them stood up to leave.

Once back outside in the car, Jenny turned to Murray.

"Well? What do you make of her?"

"Bitter. Can't say I blame her. But she didn't tell us much, could have done with seeing this Nicole. All we have is the mother's word that she is alive and what was all that about being agoraphobic? Pretty handy for someone who needs an alibi."

"Mmm. I tend to believe her on that one. Did you notice the shoes in the hallway?"

"Shoes?" Murray started his engine and checked

his mirrors as his dark green Astra pulled out and started the journey to Exeter.

"Hmm. There were some pumps like what Mrs Sampson had on, cheap and a bit tatty, and four pairs of brand new court shoes, sandals, mules and ankle boots. Rather a lot of new shoes wouldn't you say?"

"You mean, they were all Nicole's? The unworn ones?" Murray glanced at Jenny and then back at the road ahead.

"Certainly possible. I like new shoes but I wouldn't buy a whole year's worth and not wear any of them outside."

"Bugger me! You and your shoes!"

It wasn't until Jenny had been safely deposited at

Exeter St Davids train station, that Ali piped up from the rear seat.

"Murray my man!"

"Ali? I wasn't sure if you were around? Thought you might have chosen somewhere else to go!"

"Murray, you can be so mean to us sometimes."

"Hello Rita!" Murray smiled at his front passenger seat where, unseen by him, Rita was chewing her fingernails. "You know I'm only teasing!" He paused to watch the traffic as he turned back onto the main road in the direction of home. "So, did you two get a snoop around the Sampson home? And was Nicole really there or are we being conned?"

"Oh she was there Murray mate. Curled up behind her bedroom door."

"I felt quite sorry for her, she looked ever so

pitiful."

"Yeah, she's definitely of the nervous sort! She was humming to herself one minute and had her ear tight up against the door the next! Bit nuts if you ask me."

"Thanks Ali! I'll make a note of that. Was she locked in her room by her mother or do you think her hiding was down to her?"

"Oh down to her Murray. We were there before you and she was quite hysterical. Didn't want to be downstairs with strangers. I think Mrs Sampson has her hands full with that poor girl to be honest." Murray considered what Rita had said but it didn't fit with what the other girls had said. They claimed to have 'seen' Nicole. Were they just hallucinating? Someone had LSD in their toxicology report? Who

was it? He couldn't stop and check his notepad.
Chantelle? When he got home he would find out
and then give Leah another call and see if she had
heard anything about Lauren's post mortem. But
then, if they hadn't really seen Nicole, what was
going on? How had all three girls died in such
similar circumstances? Murray shook his head, Mrs
Sampson had to be lying about Nicole?

Once home Murray checked that he had
remembered rightly that it was Chantelle who had
had LSD in her system when she died and then he
picked up his phone and dialed Leah's number. Ali
and Rita had followed him indoors. Ali slumped
down on the settee and cleaned his small round
glasses on his waistcoat and Rita stood next to

Murray so to hear both ends of his phone conversation.

"Hello Leah?" Murray asked.

"Hello yes, oh, is that Mr Barber?"

"Yes it's me. I was wondering if you'd heard anything about Lauren's post mortem? It's just that one of the other girl's, Chantelle, had a hallucinatory drug in her system and I've just come from Nicole's house and, according to her mother, she's completely agoraphobic, never goes outside. I'm just trying to work out how these girls could have seen Nicole..."

"Yes. Yes I've had a conversation with the coroner and yes, there were traces of LSD in Lauren's body. Which is totally out of character for her, I mean, taking 'social drugs'. She just didn't do that. There was another thing that surprised me too, apparently she was HIV positive. I don't know how she contracted that?"

"That's interesting. Nicole is too. Her mother blamed that night on the beach but I took it she was just bitter. Maybe that's something to think about....
"

"There's one last thing as you've called Mr Barber.."

"Yeah?"

"Another one of those letters has arrived. Those nasty ones? Did you want me to e-mail it to you?"

"Yes please, or I can pick it up if you like, I've got to drive out past you this afternoon. It'd be handy to have a look at the post mark."

"Sure, I'll be in now for the rest of the day so

whenever you like."

With the call ended, Murray turned to face the centre of his empty lounge.

"Well, what do you two make of this?" he asked.

"I think we should try and communicate with the girls on our side again. Find out if they really saw Nicole or if they were just hallucinating?"

"Ok, Ali."

"Murray.." Rita was deep in thought. "If that letter has just arrived for Lauren, whoever sent it can't have known the girl was dead surely?"

"No, I suppose not? .... But that would mean, whoever sent the nasty letters has nothing to do with the girl's dying...?"

CHAPTER SEVEN

Murray stopped off at Leah's place and picked up
the new letter on his way down to his parent's
house. He had his camera equipment packed up in
his boot ready to install in the museum, hopefully it
would be a straight forward case of filming and
identifying some curious local snooping around the
artifacts during the middle of the night. Ali and Rita
had disappeared off to wherever it was they went,
Murray never asked questions like that, and said
they'd get back to him as soon as they found
anything out.

He had taken a quick glance at the letter but it was
pretty much the same as the others. It did puzzle
him however, just who was writing them? Someone

certainly had a vindictive side to their character. He made a mental note to ask all the others whether or not they had received any such letters too. The postmark on the letter that now lay beside him on his passenger seat was dated just a couple of days ago, Saturday, long after Lauren had died. The area it had been posted? Torbay. It seemed at the moment that all roads led back to Nicole. Was she really agoraphobic? Was it a twenty-four hour a day act that was even fooling her own mother?

Almost as soon as he walked in through his parent's front door, Murray was being given the third degree on his health. He tried in vain to convince his mother that he really was one hundred per cent fine but still she insisted on laying her hand across his forehead to check his temperature and gently feeling his ribs to see if he winced. He

did, but only in trying to escape from her grasp.

Once he had promised to return for a fish and chip

supper he was allowed to head down to the museum

to meet Emma Walker.

It was another dull day and the light outside was

dim. This hung darkness throughout the narrow

rooms and even though he knew things about

ghosts, Murray still felt the eeriness as he stepped

inside the seventeenth century building. There were

only the two part-time workers, Emma who did

most of the admin and Pete Thoms, who did the

physical stuff like the lifting and other general

caretaker duties. They both now stood staring at

Murray waiting for him to install the surveillance

cameras. Emma had led them through five or six

rooms filled with curiosities and old relics of local interest. They stopped in a room on the first floor which housed a number of glass topped tables encasing some shipping history and treasures brought back by long forgotten fishermen.

"This is the room we seem to be suffering the most disturbances in Mr Barber... or can I call you Murray, knowing your mother so well?"

"Murray's fine." he smiled but wondered what knowledge Emma had been given by his mother? "So, nothing's been stolen? They just keep moving things?"

"Yes, I know, it's a bit odd! They just don't put them back quite straight. In here..." she pointed at one of the tables. "... these scrolls. They're old maps, fishermen charts, with scribbled notes on, that's all."

"Not a fisherman looking for some old waters with new fish stock?" Murray attempted some humour. Emma grimaced and Pete was stood in the doorway with his arms folded... but someone found it funny, someone was laughing....

Murray set up two cameras, one covering the doorway and the other aimed at the table in question and most of that end of the room. It crossed his mind that, maybe, this was down to their unseen guest, who had now returned to silence. Would it be another case like that of Jason Castle? If it was or not, he wasn't going to strike up a conversation with any ghost in front of Emma and Pete. Perhaps he would send in Ali and Rita later?

Emma offered him a cup of tea while he worked

which he happily accepted. Maybe he could get a closer look at the scrolls himself while he drank? He glanced at the maps. He recognized the name Polperro, so they must be of the local coastline? Unfortunately, he had to admit he was no expert on any matters to do with the sea, he may have grown up in a fishing town but he had always been a land-lover! Perhaps the museum's resident ghost would know who the maps belonged to and what was so interesting about them?

"One cup of tea Murray!" Emma had returned, Pete however, had work to do and so excused himself.

"Do you know much about these maps then?" he asked as he sipped his drink.

"These? Well, they're from the early part of last

century, about 1905. They came from the 'Polmary Eugenie', a twenty-eight footer. Her skipper was Roy Tamblin but he unfortunately didn't make it back from his last trip out. The Polmary came back in pieces."

"Are these pieces of timber all that's left of her?" Murray was staring at the other artifacts within the tabletop case.

"Mmm. She'd been down into Spanish waters but just hit bad weather off the coast here and, like so many others, hit the rocks on the way in. Tamblin got washed overboard apparently."

"Dangerous way to earn a living."

"Still is Murray."

"What did she have on board? Maybe your visitor's after lost treasure?" Murray smiled at Emma but his 'humour' had caught someone else's attention again. A chuckle rang round the room.

"Fish! But you could be right, plenty of smuggling in these parts!"

With his drink finished, the two wandered to the office where Murray installed the recorder which would pick up the pictures caught by the cameras. If anything had moved overnight, he said he would come back tomorrow and check the film with her. Emma said she felt safer already and would be in touch.

Cod and chips went down well back at his parent's house and while his Mum cleared the dishes, Murray showed the new letter to his Dad and told him about his latest case.

"Not a pleasant business, is it Son?" His Dad glanced at Murray over the top of his glasses. "Do you think someone's working their way through the list of all the girls?"

"Seems like it doesn't it? But this Nicole is supposedly a total agoraphobic."

"Maybe, maybe not? But what I would be concentrating on Son, is the next victim. Who's next?"

"You mean..." Murray stared at his Dad. "You mean someone else could already be in danger now? Hadn't thought about that properly." He flicked through his notebook stopping on the list of the girls. "Hannah, Chantelle and Lauren are already dead... which leaves Clare, Abigail and Jasmine. I've spoken to Jasmine face to face and she was fine, very level-headed. I haven't been able to get hold of Abigail yet and Clare... actually Clare did sound strange. I only spoke to her on the phone, she could have been scared? They all seem to get paranoid at first and depressed but they also have drugs in their systems...."

"Is it possible that someone, say Nicole if we ignore the phobia, being able to get near enough to the victim to introduce the drugs to them, quite probably without them realizing what she's doing?"

"How do you mean Dad?"

"Well.... if they didn't recognize her maybe she would visit them somehow and leave the drugs in something in the kitchen?"

"Mmm. Sounds a bit far-fetched. Besides, the victims say they saw Nicole. Said she was coming after them." Murray flicked through his notebook again.

"I think you should do some surveillance on this Nicole. If she heads out to any of the girls homes you've got her." Murray was only half listening to his Dad, he had noticed something in his notes.

"I think I know who the next victim is Dad."

"What? Who?" His Dad sat forward.

"Jasmine said that when they passed the knife around, first it was Hannah, then Chantelle, Lauren, Clare, Abigail, Jasmine and then Nicole... Hannah, Chantelle, Lauren.... Clare's next?"

CHAPTER EIGHT

Murray didn't drive home when he left his parent's house, he filled the car with petrol and headed back to Torquay. He parked along the road from the Sampson house and waited. If Nicole was going to make a move tonight, he was going to catch her. Of course, it would be a lot easier if Ali and Rita were around, but he didn't have a direct line to call them on.

It was a cold night but he kept his window open and listened to the sound of the waves breaking somewhere below him on the cliffs. It was dark which helped hide his presence and by ten o'clock he was in luck, someone had come out of the Sampson house. It was a woman but Murray couldn't tell if it was mother or daughter as they strolled in the opposite direction down the hill.

"Boo!" Murray jumped. He then let out a loud sigh, perfect timing!

"Ali? Brilliant! Go and find out who that woman is please! Is it Nicole?" he pointed down the road at the disappearing figure.

"Ah man! Don't you want to hear what we got to say?"

"Not right now. Just follow that woman!"

"Please yourself!"

"Ali, you go, I'll stay and tell Murray what we found out." Rita's voice came from the rear seat. First glancing in his rearview mirror, Murray turned sideways and stared at the back seat.

"Rita? Sorry to sound ungrateful but I'm worried

about our next victim. I think Clare's next on the list."

"Oh dear. Has she said anything then?"

"Not a lot but they seem to be dying in the same order that they used the knife. I just want to see if Nicole is lying through her teeth about this agoraphobia. What did you find out anyhow?"

"We still haven't spoken directly with the girls but our contact says that their statements say, and I quote, 'Nicole didn't look a day different from that night on the beach'. Now, forgive me if I sound naive Murray, but I'd love not to age a day in six years. If she's still alive surely she must look different now?"

"Rita, honey, you haven't aged a day since 1976! But I see what you mean. If they thought they were

86

seeing a ghost, then she'd look the same as when she had died six years ago, or at least that's what they'd think. But she's alive, and older by six years? Maybe she doesn't look a lot different? It doesn't make sense otherwise. Could they be mistaken?" He glanced questioningly at where he thought Rita was sitting.

"Well, they say they saw her in their homes, during the night. They could have been dreaming? Filling in the gaps of what they thought they were seeing? They were on hallucinatory drugs..."

"Maybe that's how she was getting the drugs into their system? They weren't actually taking the drugs themselves, they were being fed to them in their food and the effect was that they thought they were going mad, getting depressed and paranoid... not knowing it was just because of the drugs..."

"Which they didn't know they were taking! It would start to explain their behaviour leading up to their deaths alright. Partly a disguise for their murder, making it look like suicide and partly a sadistic sort of torture, watching them suffer. If it is this Nicole, then she's very twisted."

"Well she's the only one with a motive. A couple of the girls had HIV but that may not be related?" Murray turned back and glanced out of his windscreen into the dimly lit street. "Doesn't explain the letters though? Someone sent Lauren a hate letter long after she had died?"

"Murray man, that ain't Nicole! That's the mother, Nicole's still indoors in her room, I just checked." Ali had returned, his voice blowing in through

Murray's open window.

"Oh well. So Nicole remains inside." Murray sat and thought. "You couldn't watch her all night could you? Just in case she goes out later?"

"We could. If you really want us to? What about Clare though? Hadn't someone better watch her if she's the next victim?" Rita sounded a little concerned.

"Yeah, maybe you're right? Oh what to do?" Murray was feeling tired. "Ok, I'll stay here if you could go and watch Clare? I've got an address here somewhere..." again he flipped through the notebook.

"Maybe you should go home man? You're likely to fall asleep, look at you. We'll cover them both, don't worry."

"Hahuh!" Rita let out a laugh. "Yes, we're not joined at the hip you know! Ali which do you want?"

"I don't mind sticking around here babe if you want to take this Clare?"

"Right, sorted Murray! Go home!"

Murray was up early the next morning. Still dressed in his dressing gown, he sat himself down in front of the phone with a coffee and dialed the first number.

"Hello?"

"Hello, is that Clare?"

"Yes, speaking, who is this?"

"It's Murray Barber, we spoke the other day? I'm a private investigator hired by Leah Trueman to look into her sister's death..."

"Oh yes, I remember. What do you want?" The girl sounded flustered.

"Please, I'd like to ask you some questions, it's quite important.... you could be in danger..."

"Me? oh! Err... ok, I suppose. Will you come round here or...."

"Yes, yes that will be good. Can I come this morning?" Murray was pleased as it would give him a chance to see what her house was like and whether someone could get in easily.

"Ok. Do you want my address?"

"59 Chestnut Drive? I have it. See you about half nine?"

"Oh, ok."

Murray punched the air, good! He felt like he was now able to protect the girl. He looked at his list, He could give Jasmine another quick call and ask about the letters and then he must try and get through to Abigail.

"Hello Jasmine?"

"Yes, who is it?" Jasmine was very matter of fact once more.

"It's Murray Barber, we met the other day?"

"Oh, yes, you. Sorry, I've had a late night, not with it yet."

"That's ok, sorry to bother you again but I wondered if I could just ask a quick question?"

"Sure."

"Have you ever had any hate mail? About that night on the beach? It's just that some of the other girls were getting letters and I just wondered whether you were too?" There was a pause before

Jasmine answered.

"Ok, yes. I have had some. Nasty things, but I just threw them away."

"You don't know who they were from?"

"Not a clue. Didn't actually care! Just some sick idiot!"

"Sorry to have brought it up but, well, if you get any more could you please pass them on?"

"You want them? Why? Do you think they have something to do with the other's dying?"

"Not directly, but I would like to find out who is sending them?"

"Yeah, ok then."

Next, he dialed Abigail's number. If she didn't answer this time then he'd have to go over there and try and find her in person. The line rang....

"Morning Murray my mate!" Ali's cheerful voice sprang from the settee behind Murray.

"Morning Ali, just trying to get through to Abigail again, hang on..."

"Hello?"

"Oh hello, is that Abigail Pengellis?"

"Yes. Who's this?"

"My name is Murray Barber and I'm a private investigator, I've been hired by a lady named Leah Trueman to look into her sister's recent death..."

"Oh Lauren, yes, I heard about her. Such a shame." She sounded genuinely upset, not in tears but affected none the less. "How can I help?"

"Yes, I'm sorry to have to bring it up, but this seems to go back some six years to an incident that happened during a camp on the beach..."

"Oh... yes I know what you're on about. But why should Lauren have killed herself over that? Surely that was all over and done with? Well.... well, except for the letters..."

"Letters? You've had letters too?" Murray started scribbling in his notebook.

"I've had a few but I'm afraid I haven't kept any of them, not very nice I'm afraid. Look, what happened to Nicky that night was bad, it was horrible, but if we'd known it was going to turn out like that we wouldn't have done it. No-one wanted her to get hurt let alone go and die..."

"Abigail... Nicole's not dead. Didn't you know that either?"

"Oh?... no. Oh, I'm so glad! It did haunt me a bit.

But you say she's alright?"

"She seems fine. Would you recognize her handwriting by any chance?"

"You think she wrote the letters? I suppose that would make sense? Afraid I wouldn't know her handwriting though. The thing I remember most about her was her fringe! Thick and heavy, could black out a window with it!"

"She ain't got no fringe now Murray mate!" Ali was eavesdropping.

"She had a heavy fringe you say? You obviously haven't seen her since, not if you thought she had died?"

"No, haven't seen any of them for ages."

"On that night, Abigail, what happened with the boys? They turned up early on but did they come back at all?"

"The boys?" Abigail was laughing. "No, they were told not to come back till much later. They did, but not till we had all gone home. I'm still with Mark and we still see Tyler and Ashley. They weren't in on the prank though, they never saw what happened."

"Mmm, can I ask whose idea the prank was?" Murray was tapping his pen on his desk.

"Err, Chantelle's I think... not sure, we all agreed anyhow."

"Well, thank you for speaking to me and take care, three of you have all died so far. Can I ask that if you get anymore letters you let me know?"

"Sure, if you want them?"

"Thanks, and if you think of anything that might

be relevant to these deaths, anything at all about that night, please feel free to call me.... oh, one last thing, you don't have to answer but, have you ever been tested for HIV?"

"HIV? no! Why should I?"

"I'm not sure, it might be irrelevant. Just two of the others have come up positive."

"Oh." Abigail voice had dropped, he had probably just ruined her day...

"....So Nicole didn't go out all night then?"

"Not once Murray." Rita was also in Murray's flat, she sat playing with one of her ponytails, perched up on the lounge windowsill. "Her Mum went out that one time but was back pretty quick. Probably went to the convenience store to get more ciggies!"

"What about Clare then? I suppose she had a quiet night if Nicole never went out?"

"No." There was a pause before Rita continued. "She had a visitor. A woman. Didn't see a car, she walked from the end of the street when she arrived. Broke in through the side door. It's not very security safe! Took her seconds!..."

"So who was it?"

"Not sure. Looked young with a dark fringe, well covered up though. She put something in the bathroom cabinet and then lent over the bed, staring at Clare. She didn't wake though, must sleep like a log!"

"But it couldn't have been Nicole?" Murray could feel frustration building up inside him. "One step forward and three steps back!"

"Someone is wearing a disguise to make it look like Nicole reeking revenge." Ali, who had been peering over the top of his small round glasses, now pushed them back up on his nose. "Someone who thought she was dead and made themselves to look like her six years ago."

"Someone who doesn't want to change their plans now, even if they've found out she's still alive Murray." Murray glanced from where Rita was at the window back to the settee where Ali sat.

"Bugger!" he muttered.

CHAPTER NINE

Murray got out of his car and stared at 59 Chestnut

Drive. It was a nice looking semi-detached with a brand new car sat on the driveway. Maybe this was Clare's parent's house? Clare herself turned out to be just what Murray was expecting, a nervy, flustered young woman who found it hard to follow his conversation. Her parents spent six months abroad every year and were not due back for another two months.

"... so you're saying that I could be the next victim? That I'm possibly being poisoned and then I'm going to kill myself?" Clare was sat at the kitchen table tightly clasping a mug of coffee. Murray was sat opposite her.

"If I'm right about what is going on, then quite possibly yes. I don't mean to set you off in a panic but, well, what you're feeling, paranoid, nervous,

thinking you've seen a ghost, it's all being set up.
You're being set up." He was trying to sound as
calm and reassuring as he could.

"So who's doing this? Is it Nicole?" Her eyes were
wide and dilated.

"I'm not sure. She could have an accomplice? It's
got to have something to do with what happened to
Nicole that night but we're just not quite sure how it
all fits together. Can you please do one thing for
me?"

"What? What shall I do?"

"Go to your doctor. Go today and tell him you've
been systematically fed drugs, LSD and maybe
some other stuff and you need help. Secondly, lock
this place up tight at night. Your back door needs to
be bolted. Have you got a bolt of any sort?"

"Bolts? Err... no, no nothing. What should I do? Will she get me?...."

"No, we won't let anything happen to you, don't worry." He wasn't sure if he even believed his own words, why should she in her state? "Tell you what, I've got a tool box in my carboot, I'll have a look and see what we can do and then I'm going to drop you off at the docs, ok?"

"Oh, ok. Yes, I can do that..."

So, with a make-shift but secure lock fixed to the back door, Murray drove Clare to her doctor's surgery and left her there. Hopefully she would be a little safer for now. Thing was, he wasn't sure who from?....

Once he was back home, he found his answer

phone flashing at him so checked his missed messages. The first was from Jeff, he and Kate wanted to treat him and Jenny to a meal out on Thursday night if they were both going to be available? He quickly dialed Jeff back.

"Hi mate, we'd love to be taken out for a meal, I'm sure Jen'll be here. Think we should go Dutch though..."

"No, we're asking so we're paying, no arguments! How's the Hayloft grab you? Kate wants to try it out?"

"Oh...." Ouch! Murray could have done without that, anywhere but where Michelle worked. "Sounds great! What time?"

"We'll book it for seven-ish, let you know ok? Oh.. and how's the case going? Anymore girl's dead yet?"

"Not yet thankfully but it's just getting weirder."

"How come?"

"Well... the three girls that have died so far have been killed in order that they used the knife on the beach that night..."

"Been killed? Not suicides?"

"It's complicated according to Ali and Rita. They did do the act themselves but only because they were walked through it if you know what I mean. Coerced as it were. Anyway, it seems to all keep coming back to this Nicole and that night but she's totally agoraphobic, doesn't leave the house. And then there's these nasty letters that have been sent to the other girls. But whoever sent them can't be in on the murders because they've been sending letters to the dead girls long after they've died. It's just a muddle at the moment mate."

"I have faith in you Murray! You'll sort it out before you know it. I've got a debriefing to go to so I'd better go but I'll catch you before Thursday ok?"

"Ok Jeff." Talking it through with Jeff hadn't really helped Murray. It still felt like something, some piece of the puzzle was missing....

He checked his next message, this one was from Emma at the museum. Things had been moved again. He phoned her back and said he was on his way, a distraction was probably just what he needed.

The museum was just closing when Murray arrived. Emma met him at the door and they went straight upstairs to the same table that Murray had set the cameras aimed at the day before.

"They've moved the charts again." Emma stated.

"They must be keen to find something out." Murray

took a good look and saw that she was right, the

scrolls were off centre on their stands. So what was

this person after?

"Well let's take a look at our film shall we?"

Murray offered and they headed back down to the

office. It clearly showed a local, one Callum

Barnsley, taking notes and copying the maps. Why,

they weren't sure, but they could now find out.

Emma asked Pete to go along to the pub and see if

Callum was about and whether he'd like to share his

story with them?

Half an hour later, Callum had unwillingly

returned with Pete and the four of them were sat

around the display while Callum explained himself.

"I've heard that they had gold on board, not fish. The smuggling lark was ripe back then. Anyhow, the story goes that when they hit the rocks old Roy Tamblin managed to get some of the gold into a cavern along the coast there before he got washed away as he tried to make it to shore."

"Where's this tale come from Cal?" Pete asked.

"Jonas is old Tubby's grandson, Tubby was onboard that night." He turned to fill in the blanks for Murray. "He told me, along with a bunch of us in the pub. I thought it might be worth a bit of further investigation. Might be something in it. I thought if I could pin-point the place the Polmary hit the rocks, then I could work out where this cavern might be."

"Why not just come and ask if you could have a closer look at these?" Emma was pointing at the display case.

"And have to explain myself? I s'pose now I'll have to donate anything I find to this place?"

"Well..." Emma was a little unsure. "Maybe we could look into a reward type payment for the donation of a local-interest historical find? I'll have a look amongst the small print. It would be quite exciting to have a new exhibit like that, get some local press interest and such like?" Her enthusiasm was growing.

"What have you got so far?" Murray asked hoping for some sort of divine help from the so far silent museum ghost.

"It's west of here. I was going to take the boat out

tomorrow and look for the ridge that shows on that map there." They all gazed at the map in question. "Thought it might be the ledge into the cavern that Jonas mentioned to us."

"Haven't been out on the waves for many a year now. Could quite fancy a trip back out there myself." The others didn't react but Murray couldn't help but glance around. The ghost silent no more.

"Do you fancy joining him Murray? We could add a bit onto your fee maybe?" Murray smiled back at Emma. He had three more girls who could be on someone's hit list, but he felt drawn towards the sea adventure.

"What's the weather supposed to be like tomorrow?" he asked.

"Drizzly but calm." Callum put in. "High tide's at

nine forty, can't miss it."

"Ok." He wasn't completely convinced he hadn't just lost his mind but decided to add, just for the fun of it... "Maybe old Tubby or even Tamblin himself might join us!"

CHAPTER TEN

On returning home to his flat later that evening, Murray found Jenny awaiting him with a bottle of Merlot already open and poured out. He was pleased to see her and was highly amused by the sporran that she had bought him, but not the kilt! Her trip had been a success but now she wanted to hear how his case was going, had he worked out what was going on?

He filled her in on as much as he could, not that he had all the answers, and told her about the possibility of Clare being the next victim. She had been quite concerned but Murray had other things on his mind... She pushed him off and told him to get the other bottle of wine first. As he stood in the kitchen and uncorked the bottle a whistling started.

"Ali?" he whispered turning slightly to his left.

"Sorry man, I forgot my flute! Didn't mean to interrupt your evening. Did you want us to watch over your lady friend again tonight?" For a moment,

Michelle popped into Murray's head but he pushed

her out again.

"Yes, if you don't mind? Just in case her visitor

comes back. Come and get me if you need to."

"Ok Murray, enjoy yourself!" And Ali was gone,

leaving Murray to return into the lounge to Jenny

where he had to tell her about the meal out with

Jeff and Kate on Thursday night.

"The Hayloft? It's supposed to be very nice there,

I've heard the food is great!" So with Jenny's

approval, it looked like the evening was booked.....

The following morning, Murray was up extra early.

He thought it was time he made Jenny breakfast,

even it was only toast. Besides, he had to be out of

the house by seven if he was to catch Callum before

he left on the high tide. As both he and Jenny left at the same time, Jenny heading to the office in Exeter, Murray wondered what if anything had happened at Clare's during the night? There hadn't been any sign of Ali or Rita so he supposed that all was well.

He drove straight down to the harbourside where he found Callum and Pete getting ready to set out.

"You coming too Pete?" Murray asked as he climbed on board.

"Not me, I get sea sick!" It crossed Murray's mind that maybe he did too? He had never had the chance to find out. Wrapped up and wearing life jackets, Murray and Callum set out to sea to follow the coastline in search of a ledge that may or may not exist. Suddenly Murray wondered what he was thinking of? Still, here he was and at least the sea wasn't too rough.

"I've got the co-ordinates here, it'll take us about twenty minutes before we're near enough to start searching closely. How's your eyesight?"

"Good. You really think we're gonna find anything?" Murray was holding tightly to the rail as he stood alongside Callum who was steering the vessel.

"I'm sure there's a cavern. Let's just hope there's something worth finding inside that cavern!"

They slowed the engines as they neared the marked spot on their copy of the map. Callum kept the boat facing slightly away from the coast so the current wouldn't drag them too close to the rocks. They let their eyes search the cliff face as they slowly moved along. It was slow and tiring. For over

an hour they trawled back and forth along the three

mile stretch of coastline. Each time their eyes

picking out a new shape or possibility of a ledge. On

the third time heading west, Murray heard the

sound of someone singing. Like the fishermen's

choirs found in every town, it was a song from the

sea. Was this old Tubby or Tamblin guiding them in

or just bored of their painful efforts?

"Can we get in closer over there?" Murray asked

pointing towards the cliff face where he thought the

singing was coming from.

"What can you see?" Callum called as he turned

the vessel in.

"Not sure." Murray called back, he could hardly

say he could hear it not see it!

"Look!" Callum suddenly shouted. "Is that a ledge? How the hell do we get on there?"

"I believe Tamblin was in the water when he made it into the cavern. If we can't make it we should mark the spot and attempt to reach it from the top of the cliff." Murray shouted back. Callum didn't answer, he was studying the flow of the waves and the lie of the rocks. Surely he wasn't going to attempt to reach the ledge?

"I think we can get in there. That outcrop calms the water there, look." Murray wanted to shout out to Tamblin or Tubby or whoever it was and ask for help but he wasn't going to do that unless he could see the end of his life in front of him, he was feeling pretty close but maybe not quite there....

As it happened, Callum steered them in with ease.

117

The boat bobbed and gently bumped the ledge in the calm pool that was shielded by the outcrop.

"One of us needs to get on that ledge while the other keeps the boat here."

"You want me to get across there?" Murray felt it was a daft question, he knew he wasn't capable of steering the boat.

"Tie this rope around you. You'll be fine!"

"Bugger, bugger, bugger...." Murray did as he was told, he'd come this far after all...

Inside the dark, damp, slippery cave Murray felt his way towards the back.

"If you're here how about some help?" he asked the dark space surrounding him.

"You asking me?" Came a voice back from the darkness.

"Yes, you! Tamblin or Tubby or whoever you are?"

"You can see me?" The man sounded confused.

"No, but I can bloody well hear you! Am I wasting my time here risking my life or have you hidden something here?" There was no reply. Murray wondered if the ghost had gone?

"Come down to your right..." Murray didn't speak but followed the instructions. As he slid on the slippery cave floor his instructions continued. ".. You can't see it but if you feel along the wall there, about your knee height, you'll feel a gap. It's filled with water but it's low enough inside that the lead box I put in there should still be in one piece..." Murray could feel his heart pounding in his throat as he fumbled along the cave wall. There? Was that the gap? He pushed his hand through into the space behind... Yes! He could feel the freezing cold, smooth surface of a square shape. He grabbed hold of it with both hands and carefully lifted it up and out of the hole. It was all of about six inches square but weighed what felt like a tonne.

"I think I've got it!" he shouted excitedly.

"Murray! What you got?" He could just hear Callum calling from outside the cavern. Murray shouted again.

"I think I've got it! I'm coming back out!" He stepped back, holding the heavy box close to his chest and turned towards where the voice had come from. "Mr Roy Tamblin I presume?"

"You would seem to have the advantage over me dear sir. Who might you be that crosses the line between that life and this?"

"The name's Murray Barber, private investigator! And hearer of the dead! I must thank you for your help. Do you want to tell me what's in here and how you came by it?"

"Aarh, I could do that? They got something back in that museum place but it's not what really happened... We had been to Egypt to pick up some fancy pieces, not all with paper's you understand..." Roy's Westcountry tones were low and secretive. "...we stopped off at Malaga on our way back and picked up some gold, sold some of what we had on board, but typical-like, we gets back into home waters and she goes up rough. I managed to stash some away in here before I tried to swim back into harbour... didn't make it!"

"Murray! You ok in there?" Callum was still

shouting from out on the boat. Murray turned to go

before he was assumed 'lost in a cave at sea'!

"Is there anything I can do to repay you?" he asked

his unseen companion.

"You can tell them to put my name on a bigger

piece of card in that little museum for a start!"

CHAPTER ELEVEN

Murray returned home that evening, tired and

drained but dry and fed with a pay cheque to look

forward to. The lead box had indeed contained

some old Spanish gold coins and some Egyptian

jewellery. Perhaps not worth a fortune but an exciting find all the same. Emma and Pete, among other interested locals, were thrilled and it went without saying how proud his Mum had been! Still, now the fun was over and Murray turned his mind back to the case of the series of dying girls.

His phone had two flashing messages which he listened to as he ran a bath. Both Jasmine and Abigail had received another foul letter each. He decided to give them both a quick call and ask when they had been post-dated. It turned out they had been collected and sent through a Torbay collection office, similar to the other one that Leah had found amongst Lauren's post, the previous morning... surely that meant that they had been posted the night that Murray had sat outside Nicole's house.

The only person who had gone out that night had been Mrs Sampson... 'a short trip probably to the convenience store' Rita had said... maybe the postbox? But that didn't mean Mrs Sampson had written them, they could still have come from Nicole? Murray turned off the bath taps and sat for a moment on the edge of his bath. He had to try and get his thought's clear in his head... Whoever sent the letters didn't know about Lauren's death, so... If Nicole was the 'murderer' then she couldn't have sent the letters.... but if she wasn't leaving the house and was agoraphobic then she wasn't the 'murderer' and she could be the sender of the letters? Was it possible that she was the 'murderer' and her mother was sending the letters and neither knew about what the other was doing? Murray let out a loud sigh and started to undress, he really wasn't getting anywhere.

Feeling better after his bath, Murray searched the kitchen for a bottle of wine to relax with in front of the tv. He didn't find one, only empty bottles. He made a mental note to go shopping in the morning especially as he was running low on food as well. Food? That reminded him that he was out for dinner the next night, the Hayloft... Maybe he should call Michelle? Save any awkward moments in front of Jeff, and Jenny of course. She might not be working Thursday night? Was it worth making waves beforehand? He found he was able to talk himself out of making the call with relative ease... he was just a dab hand at putting things off.

"You look like you lost something Murray mate?"

"Ali?" Murray turned around and faced the oven. "Wondered when you two were gonna show up? Has anything happened to Clare?"

"No, all quiet over there man, Rita's stayed with her just in case."

"Oh good. I think it must be either Nicole or her Mum sending these nasty letters. It all depends on who is causing these deaths... am I supposed to call them murders or not?"

"If you want. They're more murder than suicide! I have to say though man, I don't think Nicole is responsible for any of this. To be honest, I just don't think she's capable."

"You mean you believe she's not acting?" Murray leant back against the work surface. "Alright, but where does that leave us? Is she capable of writing the letters?"

"I don't think so. Her Mum would have to be in on it anyhow, she has to post them, she'd see the addresses. And as you said, the letters and the deaths ain't connected..."

"No. What if they're not connected at all? What if Mrs Sampson is writing and sending the letters, she's certainly bitter enough... But the deaths are for a totally different reason?"

"Such as?"

"The girls are dying in the same order as they used the knife, Hannah, Chantelle, Lauren and now Clare showing the same signs..."

"Why though Murray?"

"The only other reason we've got? And that means we only have a small choice of culprits.... although I suppose we should include the lads?" Murray was turning his thoughts over and over in his mind. "Hang on, where does seeing Nicole fit into this?"

"No idea mate, you lost me ten minutes ago...."

Murray tossed and turned all night. He was trying to make all his thoughts fit into his theory. Parts did, some parts he just didn't understand yet, but he was determined to get there. While he sat and had some toast for his breakfast, he jotted down a shopping list and then sent Jenny a quick text to remind her he would pick her up at six ready for their meal at the Hayloft with Jeff and Kate. He even promised her that he would not drink so be able to drive, well, he didn't want to lose his ability not to say the wrong thing in front of Jenny and

Michelle...

As he threw on his jacket and picked up his keys he was stopped from leaving for the supermarket by the phone ringing.

"Murray Barber, private investigator." It was a lady in need of his services. Her lorry driving husband had always spent a lot of time away from home but now he should be thinking about their retirement and her suspicions that something was not quite right were being raised by his evasive behaviour. She started to give a list of incidents but Murray interrupted and explained it wasn't necessary for quite so much information. He asked for the usual details and, of course, the husbands photo. She said she would send one straight away by phone message. Murray took down the lorry license plate and usual route details and promised he would be on to it that very morning. It wasn't the best of timing but he had turned down jobs the previous month due to his recovery from his accident and his bank balance was suffering, besides, jobs rarely had 'good' timing!

Murray glanced at his shopping list and then shoved it into his pocket, he'd try and pick some of it up later, he then headed out of the door in search of one Mr Robert Andrews and his lorry.

By one o'clock Murray found himself in Birmingham. Robert dropped off his lorry at a dispatch yard and after what seemed like ages chatting to a couple of other drivers, he jumped in a red hatchback with a woman driver and headed off. With one eye on the time, Murray followed the pair back to a semi-detached house where he managed

to grab some film on his phone of the two

discussing the state of the garden, 'their' front

garden, and then the cost of 'their' son's rent on his

new flat... Murray played back what he had

recorded, he had just about picked up the

conversation. Whether Robert was married to both

women or not, or if this second woman knew about

the first, he had no idea. It was a surprisingly quick

result, not a good one but a success all the same.

With any luck now he would be back home and still

have time to make the supermarket, phone Mrs

Sampson and tell her to quit her letter writing else

he'd report her to the police and get ready before

picking up Jenny...

He spent the journey back down the motorway

thinking about Abigail Pengellis and Jasmine Wills. He hadn't yet met Abigail though she had sounded very down to earth on the phone. Jasmine had seemed almost indifferent. It was hard to picture either of them participating in such a devious act, but devious was exactly how Murray described it. Planned and carried out without any remorse. To somehow enter the home of, and contaminate the foods of the victim, to allow them to believe they were being haunted, guilt-ridden by what they had thought was a fatal incident from their past. Dressed as the poor Nicole who was probably guilty of absolutely nothing amongst all of this... all to cover up the indiscriminate act of revenge against 'whoever' it was that had infected their own life. Now the question was how to find out which one?

CHAPTER TWELVE

Mrs Sampson had been very short. She had totally
denied everything but went extremely quiet when
Murray mentioned the police. He could only hope
that this would be the end of it as far as the letters
were concerned.

It was now ten to seven, he had picked up Jenny in
a black halter-neck top and trouser suit and with
what must have been six-inch heels. Murray had
managed to fit in a fresh shave and found a smart
shirt and pair of navy chinos. Jenny had been on
the phone to her Mum and she wasn't in a

particularly good mood, apparently the divorce was far from settled which left Murray without knowing the right thing to say which itself didn't help the way he was feeling about the evening in front of them.

Their table was ready for them as they entered and the young waitress sat them straight down and offered them each a menu. Murray glanced over at the bar area just as Michelle appeared from the kitchen. Their gaze met just for a split second... she hadn't looked angry? Murray stared back down at his menu but Jeff was already calling out to her to come over and 'meet the wife'.

"Thought you worked here, or rather ran the place! How are you? Haven't seen much of you since the reunion." Murray glanced up at her crisp white shirt and her soft hair which she had tied up in a plain but perfectly positioned bun exposing the back of her neck...

"I'm fine thank you. Nice to meet you." She turned to Kate who introduced herself.

"I'm Kate, 'the wife'! You must have been shocked with that murder at the school?"

"Oh yes. More in the line of these two I think, not my thing!" She smiled at Jeff and nodded towards Murray.

"This is Jenny, with Murray." Jeff continued.

"Hello." Michelle spoke in a friendly, if not professional voice.

"It must have been hell being at school with these two?"

"Oh, they were alright, most of the time!"

Everyone was laughing but Murray could feel his heart pounding inside his chest. Why hadn't he phoned her and explained about the accident? "How have you all been anyway?"

"Oh not too bad, except Murray here who had a bad car accident. Got snowed in up on the moors for a couple of days and then hit black ice on the way down and ended up in hospital for most of a week!"

"Oh no! Are you ok?" Now their eyes met and lingered. She seemed genuinely concerned.

"Yeah, it wasn't that bad really. Fractured rib, knocked myself out, nothing too serious. Wrote my car off..."

"Oh hark at him! More worried about his damn car!" joked Jenny. "You were unconscious for a day!

Could have killed yourself...." And so it seemed the evening would be ok, although Murray would be much happier if he could have a quiet word with Michelle just to explain himself.

As first their drinks, just water and fruit juice all round, and then their food arrived the topic of conversation turned to Murray's cases which helped him keep his mind, and eyes, from straying towards Michelle who appeared and disappeared during the evening from dining room to kitchen.

"...So you think you've sorted out the hate mail then?" Jeff asked between mouthfuls of seared tuna.

"I hope so. It has to be either mother or daughter but as only mother leaves the house, she has to be in on it. Now I just need to work out which girl is responsible for pushing the others over the edge."

"It's not this Nicole then?" Jeff asked.

"No, not if she doesn't leave the house as I say, no it's either Jasmine or Abigail..."

"And they're doing what exactly? Forcing suicide?" Kate sounded unsure.

"Basically. They're gaining access into the houses and placing medications and hallucinatory drugs in the girl's foodstuffs. They dress as Nicole incase they're seen. They return and do this a few times and the girls are getting more and more affected until they become totally paranoid. It's probably a bit hit and miss but I think they must just keep going until they get the desired effect from the victim. Then they take enough stuff with them to overdose on and entice the girl to take it to stop the madness. It's a lot of surmising, I could yet be proved totally wrong."

"You be careful Murray, you don't know how dangerous this person might be?" Jenny touched his hand, she must be over her conversation with her mother.

"Have you got much else on at the moment?" Kate put in.

"You mean apart from my treasure hunting sea adventures! Just been to Birmingham this afternoon and caught a bigamist!"

"Really?"

"Well, two ladies in separate cities!"

"Men! Never cease to amaze do they Jen?"

"Hey! It's women too!" Jeff wasn't going to let the evening melt into a battle of the sexes, besides, he and Kate had something serious to ask Murray and Jenny.

"We'd like to ask the pair of you to be Godparents, if you would like?" Both Murray and Jenny stared from Jeff to Kate.

"Wow? What do we have to do?" he asked.

"Not a lot mate. It's just the ceremony really. You're supposed to take charge of the child's religious welfare but we're just following tradition mainly."

"Oh I don't know, I think Murray's quite well equipped to guide our firstborn through the do's and dont's of getting into the afterlife!"

"Kate! She's just winding you up Murray. Don't take any notice, but we would like the two of you to say yes."

Murray glanced at Jenny.

"Sure, of course we will." she smiled. "As long as you both realize that we know absolutely nothing about babies and children!" she sat back having raised her eyebrows. She then picked up her juice to make a toast to the unborn child.

Towards the end of the evening, Murray excused himself to the gents. It was tucked around the corner out of site of the dining room. He stopped on the way by the door to the back kitchen where he spotted Michelle.

" 'Chelle, can we talk?"

"Yeah, sure." she shrugged and pointed out through the back door. She stood with her arms wrapped across her chest.

"I'm sorry..."

"Don't! Don't, alright. I said I wouldn't be offended if you didn't call..."

"But I was going to. I just didn't make it home." They stared at each other in silence.

"And when you did make it home you still didn't call..."

"Ok. I thought better of it... But that was before I saw you again tonight..."

"Don't! Don't mess with my head! If you hadn't come here tonight you still wouldn't have called would you?"

"Maybe not. But I did come and I have seen you."

"Look, I know I said I just wanted some fun with no strings..."

"We could still have that." But Michelle was shaking her head.

"We're both adults Murray, we know it's not that simple." She was holding his gaze now. "I know I'll fall arse over tit and I don't want to get hurt."

"What do you want me to say?.. What can I do?" Murray stepped towards her but she took a step back.

"You better get back inside before they start to wonder where you are." Murray shoved his hands into his pockets.

"Can I phone you and we can talk about this somewhere else?" he had started to head back inside the door.

"I haven't changed my number." she muttered as she turned her back on him.

CHAPTER THIRTEEN

Having said goodnight to Jeff and Kate and
dropped Jenny back at her house-share, with the
excuse that he might go and watch Clare's house
just in case, Murray headed home. Hopefully Ali
and Rita were still watching Clare for him but he
decided to give her a quick call just to make sure
she was alright. She sounded nervy still. The doctor
had taken some blood and she had to return on the
following Monday to see what was in her system.
Murray told her not to do anything silly regardless
of who might be encouraging her and told her
clearly to call him if anyone got inside the house.

He then slumped back on his settee and stared at the tv screen but not registering any of the late night film. His mind was trying to decide whether Michelle was worth it? All rational thought said leave it be but something else told him that he didn't want to let it go. He got up and went back out to his car. He drove to Michelle's terraced house and sat in his car outside. The lights were off but the tv could be seen flickering away in the front room. She was home from work.

"Murray! Why can't you stay where you can be found?" Ali was in the passenger seat beside him. "Murray my man? Hello! Come on, your girl's got a visitor, you've gotta move now man!" Murray came back to the present, he turned and stared at the empty seat beside him.

"Clare?"

"Yeah man!"

"Who is it?" he had already started up his engine as he spoke.

"Dunno. She's got a wig on and a photo, life-size like, tied to her face..."

"A what?"

"Like a mask. A blown up photo of that Nicole. That must be why they keep saying it's Nicole they see."

"They've gone to a lot of trouble whoever they are." He pulled up outside the front gate and ran up the path. Knocking on the door loudly, his last thoughts were about waking up the neighbours.

"Rita's inside, I'll go check what's happening." Ali's voice disappeared through the front door.

"Who's making that racket? People are trying to sleep!" A voice shouted from the upstairs window of a neighbouring house.

"Call the police!" Murray shouted back and then made his way around the side of the house to the back door, trying to see where the intruder had got inside.

"Murray! The back window! She's still in there. She was heading upstairs, I reckon she was going to finish her tonight..."

"Surely if she's heard me she'll just try to escape won't she?...."

Some three quarters of an hour later, Murray was sat in the front room of Clare's house along with Clare, an officer and the unseen Ali and Rita.

Another two officers were interviewing the now unmasked Jasmine Wills in the kitchen. They could hear her voice coming through the rooms as she protested as to how 'one of those bitches ruined her life. She'd found out she was HIV two years before and that's when she started putting together her plan of revenge. People might live with HIV but it affected every decision you made, telling boyfriends and watching them run...' on and on she ranted. She had worked her way through the list of girls to make sure the guilty one paid for destroying her future.... it wasn't pleasant to listen to...

Jasmine was finally taken into custody and with a neighbour taking Clare over to their house for the night, Murray was free to go home. It was now gone two in the morning. As he drove along he couldn't decide which way to go, home or Michelle's? Would

she still be up? Unlikely. Going over to Jenny's

house-share wasn't an option he considered and the

thought of his empty flat? That was the last place he

really wanted to go. He headed back to Michelle's, if

the tv was still on he just might knock.......

L - #0101 - 090719 - C0 - 210/148/8 - PB - DID2561280